DETECTIVE ZACK
A Christmas Mystery

JERRY D. THOMAS

Pacific Press Publishing Association
Boise, Idaho
Oshawa, Ontario, Canada

Edited by B. Russell Holt
Designed by Dennis Ferree
Cover and inside art by Kim Justinen
Typeset in 13/16 New Century Schoolbook

Library of Congress Cataloging-in-Publication Data:

Thomas, Jerry D., 1959-
    Detective Zack and the Missing Manger Mystery / Jerry D.
Thomas.
        p.   cm.
    Summary: Zack investigates the mystery of what has hap-
pened to the manger for the church's Christmas nativity scene,
along with other puzzling occurrences, while discovering the
real meaning of Christmas.
    ISBN 0-8163-1234-6
    [1. Christmas. 2. Christian life. 3. Mystery and detective sto-
ries.]   I. Title. II. Series: Thomas, Jerry D., 1959-   . Detective
Zack ; 4.
PZ7.T366954De   1994
[Fic]—dc20   93-41480
                                                       CIP
                                                        AC

94 95 96 97 98 ● 5 4 3 2 1

Dedication

To the teachers and parents who will take
time this year to use angel wings, shepherd
costumes, and overactive children to tell
the story of God's love.
And to the fathers who will once again be
called upon to share their bathrobes.

Other books by
Jerry D. Thomas

Contents

CHAPTER ONE

Back in the Bathrobe Again

December 15

Maybe it's just me, but I think it's hard to look like a wise man with a chicken sitting on your head.

Let me explain.

This time every year, my church does a Christmas program. It's always held on Christmas Eve and everyone in the community is invited. Well, this year, my mom's in charge of the program.

That should tell you right away that I'm in trouble.

Every time my mom plans a program, she wants me to be in it. Now, don't get me wrong—I don't mind being in a choir or a play sometimes. But I've worn every bathrobe I've had since I was four in a Christmas program.

At first, you get to be one of the shepherds. Not one who actually goes to see Baby Jesus, just one who gets to wear a bathrobe and sing in the shepherd-and-angel choir.

Then, when you're older, you get to be an important shepherd—you still wear your bathrobe, but they let you carry a stick. Or staff or cane or whatever they call it. And then you get to act out the Bible story. You walk up to Joseph and Mary (you hope they've stopped fighting about who gets to sit next to the manger) and kneel down to look at the plastic doll lying on the hay.

I guess the same thing happens to girls. My sister Kayla said, "If I have to wear a white choir robe and sing in the angel choir once more, I'm going to scream." That would have broken the "silent night," for sure.

"At least you don't have to wear the same thing you wear in the bathroom," I told her.

But she wanted to work her way up too. "I want to be an important angel. I want to announce good news to the shepherds. I want to wear angel wings!"

Finally, she got promoted to one of the angels who appear to the shepherds. Wings and everything. I guess the only thing left for girls after that is to be Mary and hold the baby. I know Kayla is working on it.

But for boys, the next big step is becoming a wise man. You know a wise man is more important than a shepherd for two reasons:

First, you can have as many shepherds as you need, but there can be only three wise men.

And second, you don't have to wear your bathrobe anymore. A wise man is so important, you get to wear your father's bathrobe.

I've never wanted to be Joseph. I mean, you just stand there. And if you're unlucky, they'll want you to hold the doll, and you'll have to, because it's supposed to be Baby Jesus.

Besides, you never know about Joseph and Mary. Sometimes the person in charge thinks little Josephs and Marys are cute. Then you end up with a Mary who holds Baby Jesus by one leg and tries to get in the manger herself.

Anyway, I've been a shepherd; I've been a wise man. This year, I told my mom I would be happy just to help behind the scenes. But, no, she had other plans for me.

We were having supper when she made the big announcement. "Well, we're going to do it. This year, the Christmas pageant is going to be different."

"How?" Kayla asked.

DETECTIVE ZACK

"This year, we're going to have a live Nativity scene. With real animals."

"That's great!" Alex shouted. He's my brother. "But what's a natibity?" He's only seven.

"Nativity [nuh-tiv-it-tee]," Mom corrected him. "Some people call it a créche [cresh]. It's a scene showing Baby Jesus in the manger. And we'll have shepherds with real sheep, a real donkey, and maybe a cow."

Dad's eyebrows went up. "Does Mrs. Hopkins know about this? You know how she feels about the manger."

Mom sounded a little nervous. "Well, not yet. But the pastor and the church board approved it."

Dad shook his head, but he was smiling. I thought a live Nativity sounded like a good idea.

That was before I found out about the chicken.

The next afternoon after school, everyone who wanted to be (or whose parents wanted them to be) in the Christmas program met at the church. When we drove up, some of the church people were building the stable in the grass near one corner of the parking lot.

"It may not look like Bethlehem yet," Pastor Vargas said, "but it will. There seems to be a lot of interest in the program this year. The fellowship hall is filling up fast."

A car pulled up behind us while they were talking. Mrs. Hopkins wasted no time getting out and marching over. She glared at the stable. "This is what you'll use to protect the manger?"

Mom spoke softly. "This is what we'll use to tell the story of Jesus' birth. The manger will be a big part of it."

"You do realize what our manger is worth, don't you? My great-grandmother bought it in Bethlehem more than eighty years ago." Mom and Pastor Vargas nodded. They had heard the story many times. "I've just brought it back from the furniture shop. I had them add another coat of varnish to protect it." She lifted the manger, wrapped in a heavy black blanket, out of her back seat and handed it to Mom.

"When Mrs. Abernathy directed the Christmas programs, we never had this kind of program. We always had the Nativity scene inside the church, like God intended."

"Now, Mrs. Hopkins," Pastor Vargas said, "God allowed the first Nativity to happen in a stable. I think it will be acceptable to have ours outdoors as well. Is your husband bringing the hay?"

Mrs. Hopkins just frowned. "Yes. He should be here by dark. I have spoken against the idea of using our manger for this program. But I have not been listened to. Mark my words—we will all regret this mistake."

She stomped off and drove away. Mom shook her head. "Don't worry about it," Pastor Vargas said. "Why don't you leave the manger here for now? I want to see how it fits in when the stable is done." He set the manger against the back wall.

We headed for the fellowship hall, where all the kids were supposed to meet. But when we opened the door, it sounded like a zoo!

Through all the barking, meowing, clucking, and shouting, I counted eight dogs, three cats, two chickens, a rabbit, and a goose. Mom ran right out into middle of it all. "Please, everyone, grab your pet and sit down. Sit!" she shouted. Finally, it started to quiet down.

Luke came in behind us. Luke's my good friend from Thunder Mountain Camp.* His family moved to our town this fall. We sat on the side away from most of the animals. "I thought this was a Christmas program, not a pet show," he said. "What's going on?"

Before I could answer, Mom spoke up. "I'm glad to see so many of you here today. I am sorry that

---

* You can read about the adventure Zack and Luke had at Thunder Mountain Camp in the book *Detective Zack and the Mystery at Thunder Mountain.*

someone gave you the idea you should bring your animals." She glared at my brother, Alex. He tried to hide behind a German shepherd.

"We are having animals in our program this year," she said, "but only animals from the story. There will be a donkey, a cow, and two sheep. That's all. No other animals."

"But can't we have one dog?" a little girl asked. "Bobo wants to be in the program so bad." She looked like she was going to cry. Bobo didn't look too happy either.

"I'm sorry," Mom answered, "only Bible animals. We'll be having the program out by the parking lot. You probably saw church members there building our Christmas stable. First, we need to find our shepherds."

Luke and I sat and waited while Mom decided who would be shepherds and angels and which lucky ones would be Joseph and Mary. While we waited, we watched Bobo staring at a white cat and licking his lips. The white cat wasn't afraid. It was too busy staring at the rabbit and licking its whiskers.

"This is asking for trouble," Luke warned in a whisper.

I'll say this about Luke. When he's right, he's right.

CHAPTER TWO

A Chicken and a Missing Manger

December 15

Finally, Mom was ready to announce her choices. "I'm asking Kayla to play the part of Mary." There was a hum of disappointed sighs. "I want Mary to ride in on the donkey, and Kayla knows how to ride. At least, she knows how to ride a horse."

Kayla stood and bowed. "Thank you, thank you very much. I'd like to say . . ." She saw Mom's glare and sat down.

"I want Joseph to be played by . . . Joseph!" Kayla rolled her eyes, but it seemed like a good idea to me. Joseph was in her class, and he was big enough to hold on to a donkey. At least long enough to call for help if the donkey starting acting like . . . well, like a donkey.

DETECTIVE ZACK

Mom went on to point out the shepherds and angels. "What about the wise men?" someone asked.

She pointed over in our direction. "I want those three to be the wise men."

I looked at Luke. "Is she talking about us?"

Mom spoke up again. "Zack, I want you three to be the wise men. I'll explain why later."

"Three?" Luke whispered. "There's only two of us." Then we looked over our shoulders. There, leaning against the wall, was Jodie.

Jodie is in our class too, but she isn't what you would call a friend. The truth is, she's a pain. She thinks she's the best at everything—basketball, soccer, baseball—everything. "I'm the fastest runner in the school," she brags.

What really makes me mad is that she's right.

Jodie rolled her eyes like the play was the dumbest ever. "I heard her tell Jenna that she'd rather be hit by a truck than be in the Christmas program," Luke whispered again. "Why is she even here?"

"She can't be a wise man," a first-grader piped up. "She's a girl."

"They're going to be our three wise persons," Mom said firmly. "I'm sure that girls were just as wise as boys in those days."

A Chicken and a Missing Manger

Luke couldn't resist. "I wonder what happened to girls since then?" he shouted.

That started a whole new round of shouting and arguing. Then it happened. For a second, I thought the room had exploded.

I don't know if Bobo lunged at the white cat, or if the white cat leaped at the rabbit. But in about half a second, the room exploded into motion. The dog was running, the cat was running, the rabbit was leaping, and then every animal in the place was moving at top speed. Along with most of the kids.

Luke and I backed away and ended up against the wall next to Jodie. I could see Alex hanging on to the German shepherd's collar and sliding across the floor. Mom grabbed at the rabbit and almost caught the cat. I heard this strange whirring sound, then a thud from over our heads.

Before I could move, one of the chickens dropped onto my head. I just stood there. What are you supposed to do with a chicken on your head? Dance?

Luke and Jodie were laughing so hard they had to lean against the wall to keep from falling down. The chicken stood up. *Buck, buck, buckaw!*

I was just hoping it wouldn't do the other things chickens do besides lay eggs.

DETECTIVE ZACK

"Zack, don't just stand there. Help!" Mom shouted.

I grabbed the chicken by both feet and held on while it squawked and flapped its wings in my face. Luke grabbed at the rabbit as it raced by him. He missed and bit the carpet.

Jodie rescued Alex by wrapping her arms around the German shepherd that was dragging him across the floor. Mom helped the little girl catch Bobo. Then Pastor Vargas and the other men came in to help. Finally, we got everyone's pet back to its owner and every owner back to its parent's car.

"Thank goodness, that's over," Mom said. Then she turned around and looked at the room. "Oh no!"

It was a disaster. Chairs were knocked over, papers were scattered everywhere, and it looked like half the kids had forgotten their coats and hats.

Sniff, sniff. "What's that awful smell?" Kayla asked.

"Take a wild guess," Mom answered, pointing to several suspicious spots left by the less well-trained animals.

Luke's parents drove up. "Oh, I'm sorry, but I have to go now," he said with a smile.

A Chicken and a Missing Manger

"Chicken!" I called him.

"Buck, buck, buckaw!" he crowed as he left.

"I have to go too," Jodie said. Then she disappeared out the door.

"I'll help," the pastor said as the others left. "Mr. Hopkins and his men are unloading the hay now anyway." We scrubbed and cleaned until he and Mom were satisfied.

"I'll call your dad and explain why we're late," Mom told us. "Get your stuff together so we can go."

Pastor Vargas had one more idea. "All we need is some of that air freshener from the storage closet," he said, "and the room will be as good as new."

Whaaoo, whaaooo! Right after he left, a firetruck began wailing in the distance. We all went over to the window to watch for it.

"It's getting louder," Alex said. Then we saw it racing down the street toward us. "I wonder where the fire is?"

"It must be close by," Kayla said. Then the firetruck slowed and turned into the church parking lot. "Really close by!"

"Look!" I shouted. "There's the fire!" We could see flames rising up in the darkness across the parking lot. "What's over there to burn?"

Then it hit me. "The Christmas stable!" I raced out the door and ran after the firetruck.

By the time Pastor Vargas and Mom got there, the fire was out. "It was just a small fire. It looks like someone piled papers outside against the back wall and lit them. Luckily, your hay is stacked inside," a firefighter told them.

I waved my hand. "How do you know someone lit some papers, if the fire burned them up?"

The firefighter looked at me. "Good question. In this case, the fire didn't burn up all the paper. There were still a few edges and scraps that didn't burn."

"Can I see them?" I asked.

He shrugged and handed one of the big pieces to me. "It was probably a bum or homeless person who picked up some trash and lit it to try to keep warm. Then when he heard the siren, he took off. Still, it's a good thing you called as quickly as you did."

"But I didn't call," Mom said.

"I did," a man called. He walked over to join us. "I'm Paul DuCaut," he said. "My wife and I saw your fire from our house next door and phoned the fire department. What are you people building over here anyway? You're not thinking of keeping animals on the church grounds, are you?

This close to my house?"

"No, no, this is our Christmas stable. For Christmas this year, we're going to have a live Nativity scene."

"And you're going to have it right here?" Mr. DuCaut asked. "That may not be such a good idea."

"Why not?"

"You'll see," was all he would say as he left.

I looked at the paper scrap. Even as sooty as it was, I could see that it was a light-blue-with-speckles color of paper. It wasn't like a newspaper or magazine kind of paper. It looked like a nice piece of stationery.

Suddenly, Pastor Vargas jumped. "The manger! Where is the manger?" We all ran around to look inside the stable. Nothing was there except the bales of hay stacked against the walls.

"Are you sure it was still here?" Mom asked. "Maybe one of the men helping you carried it into the church."

Pastor Vargas took a deep breath. "Maybe so. Let's check inside the church before we panic."

But the manger was nowhere to be found.

See how complicated things are? I haven't even had a chance to tell you why I'm writing in my notebook this time.

CHAPTER THREE

What's Santa Got to Do With It?

December 16

"Boy, was Mrs. Hopkins hopping mad."

The next day after school, I was telling Luke what happened at the church after he left. We were shooting baskets outside while we waited for my mom. "She's sure that someone stole the manger and sold it to get the money."

"It's not going to be much of a Nativity scene without a manger," Luke said.

"We can probably make another one, but it won't be the same. That antique one has been used in our church at Christmas for a long time. Besides, I don't like the idea of someone taking that manger right out from under our noses. And what about that fire?"

DETECTIVE ZACK

"Oh no." Luke clunked a shot off the backboard. "It sounds like Thunder Mountain again. Another mystery to solve."

I chased down the ball and agreed. "We have to get down to the church this afternoon. There have to be some clues about what happened." I bonked one off the rim.

Luke shivered and let the ball bounce right past him. "See, we can't even make a shot. It's too cold out here. If we stay out much longer, I'm going to be frozen solid."

"It is cold," I agreed. "But, really, I wish it would snow." Luke looked at me like I was crazy. "Not right now. But before Christmas. I like having snow at Christmastime." Then an idea bounced out of my brain. I grabbed the ball and held it.

"What if Mrs. Hopkins is just pretending to be mad? What if she took the manger to keep us from having the program?"

"Would she do that?" Luke asked. I shrugged my shoulders.

We were still there shooting (well, I was shooting—Luke was mostly shivering) when a white van rolled up in front of the school. Written on the side in big letters was "MCKANE MUSIC."

Luke and I both turned to look just as Jodie dashed out of the school and jumped in the van.

"Where is she going in such a hurry?" Luke asked as the van pulled away. "And who is she going with?"

"I think that was her dad's van. He runs a music store. Maybe they were in a hurry."

Luke finally talked me into going inside. We waited in the school lobby by the front doors. "My mom's talking to Mrs. Lin about the program," I explained. Mrs. Lin is our teacher. We always dropped Luke off on our way home, so he had to wait too.

My sister, Kayla, popped out of a classroom and collapsed onto the floor beside us. "I can't wait to be in the pageant. I've been waiting for years to be Mary."

"We might not even have the play without the manger," I muttered. "And it wouldn't break my heart if we didn't."

"Being in the play doesn't seem so bad," Luke said. It was my turn to look at him like he had lost his mind. "Well, it could be fun, dressing up in robes and everything." He jumped up on one of the lobby chairs. "Hark, hark, hark . . . What else does the angel say?"

I laughed. "You sound like a dog with a speech problem!" Kayla was practically rolling on the floor.

DETECTIVE ZACK

"Ahem!"

We all whipped around to see Mrs. Antonelli, the principal. "Luke, perhaps you would be more comfortable sitting in that chair." He stepped down quickly and sat up straight.

"Yes, ma'am."

She looked at Kayla and me. "We placed chairs here in the lobby so those who were waiting could sit in them." We jumped up and sat like Luke.

"Yes, ma'am."

Mrs. Antonelli tried not to smile, but her eyes twinkled anyway. "Now, have any of you seen my flashlight?"

We knew just what she was talking about. Whenever we saw Mrs. Antonelli around the school, she always had two things with her—a big ring of keys and a short black flashlight. She said it was her job to be prepared if anything should happen.

"Just this once, I think I left it on my desk," she went on. "But when I came back from the cafeteria a moment ago, I couldn't find it."

Her office was down the hall. "I haven't seen it," I answered. "And I haven't seen anyone go in your office since we've been here." Kayla and Luke nodded.

Mrs. Antonelli shook her head. "I guess I could

have left it down in the furnace room in the basement. Well, let me know if you happen to see it." With that, she turned and walked back to her office.

I don't know who thought it first, but Luke and I looked at each other at the same time. "What about Jodie?" he whispered.

"Maybe she was running out because she had just grabbed Mrs. Antonelli's flashlight off her desk," I hissed back.

"What are you guys whispering about?" Kayla asked. "Do you know something about the flashlight?"

Before I could answer, my mom and my brother, Alex, walked up. "Are you ready to go?" Mom asked.

While we were walking out, I tried to remember exactly what I had seen. I nudged Luke. "Was Jodie holding anything when she ran out of the school?"

Luke shrugged. "I didn't see anything. But she could have had it under her coat. Do you really think she would steal Mrs. Antonelli's flashlight?"

I shook my head. "Who knows? She's never been in any unusual trouble at school. But once, I overheard Mrs. Antonelli tell Mrs. Lin that there was some problem at her home. Anyway, let's keep our eyes open."

Mom didn't have time to go by the church, so I was stuck at home thinking about the missing manger. Then my friend Bobby gave me something else to think about. You remember Bobby. He's the one who told me that Noah's flood didn't really happen and that the stories in the Bible were just fables.

Of course, since then, I have seen clues about Noah's flood in rocks. And I've seen the real places in Israel and Egypt where the Bible stories happened.*

After telling Bobby all about it, he seemed more interested in God and the Bible. That's why I was kind of surprised at something he said. We were climbing a tree in the woods between our houses.

"Zack, what's happening for Christmas at your house? Are you going to your grandparents' house or something?"

"Not for Christmas," I answered. "We have a Christmas pageant at our church on Christmas Eve. My mom's the person in charge of the program."

---

* This all happened in Zack's first adventure, *Detective Zack and the Secret of Noah's Flood.*

What's Santa Got to Do With It?

Bobby looked at me with squinted eyes. "Your church is having a program about Santa Claus?"

"No." I laughed. "It's about the night Jesus was born. That's what Christmas is about, isn't it?"

"I thought Christmas was about getting presents," Bobby said. "You know, stockings hung up by the chimney and flying reindeer and Christmas trees and lots of food to eat."

I didn't tell Bobby, but the more I thought about it, the more it seemed like he was right. If Christmas was about Jesus, then where did Santa Claus come from? And Christmas trees and stockings and lights strung all over people's houses?

And why do you hear a lot more about Santa and presents than you do about Jesus?

Later, after supper, Dad said, "Zack, I have to run down to the church for a few minutes. Want to come?"

Did I ever.

> **"Is Christmas about Jesus being born, or is it about getting presents and decorating the Christmas tree?"**

Words to Remember

Nativity: a scene of Baby Jesus in the manger, with Mary and Joseph and all the shepherds and wise men (wise people).

Créche: another word for a Nativity scene.

Christmas Clues

What is Christmas really all about? If it's about Jesus being born in Bethlehem, what do Santa and lighted trees and presents have to do with it?

Missing Manger Mystery

There was a fire at the stable. And the church's manger is missing. Mrs. Hopkins is sure it was stolen.

What if she took it to protect it? And to stop the Christmas program?

What did Mr. DuCaut mean about the Christmas program not being a good idea?

CHAPTER FOUR

Clues in the Dark

December 17

I grabbed my hat and my flashlight and headed for the garage. Finally, I had a chance to look for clues at the church. On the way there, though, I had a different question.

"Dad, what is Christmas really all about?"

He stared ahead at the oncoming headlights. "That's a good question."

Just then, we drove by a billboard showing a decorated tree and people drinking and partying. The words underneath said, "It's beginning to look a lot like Christmas."

He glanced over at me. "A lot of people think it's about decorating and partying."

I pointed to a store window filled with wrapped

Christmas presents. "A lot of people think it's about getting as many toys as you can. It's confusing."

We drove into the church parking lot, right by the dark Christmas stable. "Bobby thinks Christmas is about Santa Claus and stockings and reindeer and stuff. He didn't know it had anything to do with church. Or Jesus."

Dad looked sad. "Zack, we believe that Christmas is a holiday celebrating the birth of Jesus."

"Was He born on December twenty-fifth?" I asked.

He shrugged. "No one knows exactly when He was born."

I went on. "And where did the Santa Claus idea come from? And the Christmas tree? None of that is from the Bible, is it?"

"Those are all good questions," Dad said. Then he smiled. "What we need is someone who can search for answers. It looks like a job for a good detective."

So that's when I decided to start this notebook. If there are clues about the real meaning of Christmas and where all these other things came from, I want to find them.

Dad went into the church, and I took my flashlight and headed for the stable. The first thing I looked at was the corner that was burned. It was on the back side, away from the parking lot, close to the DuCauts' house.

The firefighters' boot prints were locked in the frozen mud. *Maybe there are other footprints*, I thought. My breath puffed out in small clouds as I circled the stable, shining the light in front of me.

The only thing I discovered was that my flashlight batteries were dying. I went around again, a little farther away from the building. "Aha!" Even with my light getting dimmer, I saw it.

Stuck in the bare twigs of a small bush was a half-burned piece of paper. It must have been part of the bunch that had been piled against the wall to start the fire.

I held it up close to my light and inspected it. It was the same light-blue-with-speckles stationery that the firefighter had shown me. But this piece had writing on one corner.

"Only part of this word is left," I said out loud. All I could see were the letters *M-E-N-T-S*. On the line below that, I could read two words: *STATE STREET*.

Maybe it was just some trash that the person starting the fire picked up. Or maybe if I knew where this stationery came from, it would be a

3 — D.Z.M.M.M.

clue. I stuck it in my pocket.

Now, what about the manger? If someone stole it, they might have left footprints or marks. I went inside the stable and shone the light around. The flashlight's light was getting dimmer, but I could see that there was nothing in the building except the stacked bales of hay.

The manger disappeared when the pastor and everyone were inside chasing animals and cleaning up. And that's when the hay was delivered. By Mr. Hopkins! He could easily have loaded up the manger and taken it home to his wife.

"But there's still the fire," I said out loud. "I don't think Mr. or Mrs. Hopkins would have started a fire. Someone who knew what the manger was worth could have stolen it and started the fire, hoping we would think it had burned up." I was beginning to think Mrs. Hopkins was right.

Then, from across the parking lot, I thought I heard a church door open. "I'm out here, Dad," I called. With my pitiful flashlight, I couldn't see if anyone came out. "Dad?"

There was no answer. I turned off my light and stepped back into the stable's shadow. I couldn't see anything, but I heard something very strange.

It was coming from the DuCauts'. It was a sliding, scaly kind of sound, like a forty-foot snake would make if it were crawling across your roof. Then, against the street light at the corner, I saw it.

Something (or someone) was standing on the DuCauts' roof!

Suddenly, I felt certain that my dad was ready to go. Even without a good flashlight, I raced across the parking lot to where our car was parked. Thankfully, Dad was just coming out the church door.

"There you are, Zack. Ready to go?"

I hopped in the car as I asked, "Dad, did you open the church door around that side a few minutes ago?"

"No, Zack. I've been in the church office since I went in. Why?"

"I thought I heard that door open. Maybe I was just hearing things." Then I remembered what I had seen. "Dad, drive over by the stable, will you? I want to see something."

We cruised past it slowly. I didn't see anything strange. The DuCauts' house looked normal. *Did I really see anything?*

When I told Luke about it the next day, I still wasn't sure. "Who would be coming out of the church at that time of night?" I asked. "If my dad didn't see anyone, no one was there, right?"

Luke wasn't so sure. "Someone could have been there. Hey, someone took the manger without being seen the other night, didn't they? And that's when the pastor and a lot of people were around. Are you sure you saw something on the DuCauts' roof?"

I frowned. "I was sure. I am sure I heard something very strange. Something is going on there. We'd better keep our eyes open."

In social studies that day, Mrs. Lin said, "Christmas traditions, the things people do to celebrate Christmas, can be very different. I want to hear about the Christmas traditions in your families."

Several kids raised their hands. I pulled out my notebook in case there might be clues about what Christmas really means.

Luke said, "My grandma always says, 'Christmas is about helping others.' Every year, she makes food for a poor family or helps at a kitchen for the homeless. We always help if we're at her house for Christmas."

Jenna said, "Every Christmas, my parents get together with some of their friends and dress up in those old kinds of clothes. You know, with the tall hats and big skirts and stuff? Anyway, then they go around the neighborhood singing Christmas carols. It's so embarrassing."

Mrs. Lin smiled. "It may seem embarrassing to you, but caroling is an old English Christmas tradition. People in Great Britain would sing and ask for money to help the poor. But when children sang, they got to keep the money for themselves."

"Good idea! I like that!"

People were whispering all over the room, until Mrs. Lin said, "OK, that's enough. Brandon, you had your hand up."

"Every Christmas Eve, my family sits around the Christmas tree, and my dad reads ' 'Twas the Night Before Christmas.' Then he reads the Christmas story from the Bible."

From my desk, I could see Jodie roll her eyes and hear her mumble something.

"Does anyone know the real name of that famous Christmas poem?" Mrs. Lin asked. No hands went up. "It was probably written by Clement Moore in 1822, and its actual title is 'An Account of a Visit From St. Nicholas.' Jodie, did you want to share a Christmas tradition with us?"

Jodie stared angrily for a second. Then she said, "Our family doesn't have any Christmas traditions. December twenty-fifth isn't much different from any other day."

DETECTIVE ZACK

If she hates Christmas so much, then why does she want to be in the Christmas program? And then I remembered something. She left the program practice at the same time Luke did a couple of nights ago. But I didn't see anyone there to pick her up. *I wonder where she went?*

"Christmas is about helping others."

Words to Remember

 Traditions: special things people do every year for Christmas or some other holiday.

Christmas Clues

 Caroling is an old English Christmas tradition. People would sing and ask for money to help the poor.

Missing Manger Mystery

 I found another scrap of paper behind the stable. This one has words on it—M-E-N-T-S and STATE STREET.

 Mr. Hopkins could have taken the manger back to his wife after he unloaded the hay.

 Someone could have stolen the manger and lit the fire to trick us into thinking it had burned up.

 I think someone else was in the church last night. But I'm not sure.

 I know I heard something strange at the DuCauts'. It sounded large and scaly, like a snake. I'm not certain, but I think I saw something or someone on their roof.

CHAPTER FIVE

Christmas Trees and Camels

December 18

"Class," Mrs. Lin said, "your assignment is to research the Christmas traditions of three other countries. Find out how and when they celebrate. Your reports are due the day before Christmas break."

"How are we going to find out those things about other countries?" Luke grumbled at lunchtime.

"Mom could take us to the library one day after school," I told him. "Never mind that now—did you see Jodie's parents pick her up the other night after practice?"

"No, I never saw them. I wonder how long she stayed around outside the church."

"I was wondering that too. Maybe she saw whoever lit the fire."

Luke swallowed another bite of his sandwich. "She probably wouldn't tell us if she did."

That didn't make sense. "Why not? She's in the play too."

Luke shrugged. "But she doesn't want to be. Jenna told me that Jodie's dad is making her be in it." Then he snapped his fingers. "I forgot to tell you something I found out about Mrs. Antonelli's flashlight."

"I hope hers works better than mine does, wherever it is," I mumbled.

Luke ignored me. "Jenna told me that Jodie was in trouble that day. Near the end of school, the janitor caught her playing with some matches. She got sent to the principal's office."

"So?"

"So, she was in Mrs. Antonelli's office. And she was mad enough to take something. Maybe Mrs. Antonelli didn't notice it was gone until later."

Then something snapped in my brain. "Did you say matches?"

Luke's eyes got big. "Are you thinking what I'm thinking you're thinking?"

"Jodie acts like she hates Christmas. And if she was playing with matches . . . wait a minute."

I dug around in my backpack. "Remember I told you that the firefighters said someone had piled papers up and lit them? Well, I found another piece of that burned paper."

"So?"

"This one has some writing on it." I showed it to him. "I think it's some business stationery or something."

He shook his head. *"M-E-N-T-S* on *STATE STREET.* We could look for a place that prints docuMENTS."

"Or a photo shop that helps you remember your happy moMENTS," I added.

"Or it could still just be trash," he said. "And State Street goes all the way across town. There must be hundreds of stores on it—too many to search through. And, the paper might not even be from this town."

I started to say something else, but he interrupted. "I know, I know. We'll have to keep our eyes open."

That evening, Kayla and I went to the mall with Mom. She had to shop for program props. You know—angel wings, shepherd staffs, that sort of thing. *I hope she looks for a few Christmas presents while she's shopping.*

For a while, Kayla and I just wandered around,

looking in stores. Then I got thirsty, so I bought an orange drink at the Nut Hut. "Look," Kayla said when we sat down, "there's Santa. You should go tell him what you want for Christmas."

I watched the little kids who were standing in line to see the man in the Santa suit. "Maybe I should. Mom's so busy with this program, she'll probably forget to shop for us at all."

I saw the Santa man look over at us, so I smiled and waved. I don't know if he smiled back or not. And his lap was full of two kids both talking at the same time, so he couldn't have waved. But when they got down, he motioned for me to come over.

"I'll be right back," I told Kayla.

"Where are you going?"

"To see Santa." The next kid in line was busy crying, so I walked right up to Santa.

"Hi, kid. I'm Santa," he said.

I laughed. "Hi, Santa. I'm Zack."

"Zack, all this ho, ho, hoing makes me as thirsty as a farmer in a field full of weeds. If I give you a dollar, will you bring me one of those orange drinks?"

"Sure." I bought the drink and delivered it to him. "Here you go, Santa. Always glad to help a man in a big red suit."

"Thanks, Zack. There'll be an extra lump in

your stocking for this."

We walked on by a store that sold Christmas-tree ornaments. "Look, Zack," Kayla said, "these ornaments are all made out of pine cones. I could do that."

I tried to ignore her and the store, but a sign in the window caught my attention. It said, "Why we decorate trees at Christmas."

Of course, I had to read it. It said, "The tradition of decorating an evergreen tree for Christmas began in Germany about four hundred years ago. It probably started because of a popular play that described an evergreen tree decorated with apples.

"The first Christmas trees were decorated with fruits, nuts, lighted candles, and paper roses. Later, painted eggshells, cookies, and candies were also part of the holiday tree trimming.

"The tradition of decorating Christmas trees came to America with German settlers in Pennsylvania in the early 1800s. Since then, the tradition has spread over much of the world.

"Often, a bright star is placed at the top of the tree. It represents the star that the wise men followed to Bethlehem."

I shook my head. "That explains where Christmas trees started. And I guess it has a little bit to do with the birth of Jesus."

When we got home, the red light on the answering machine was blinking. Dad pushed the button. *Beep.* "Hi, this is Pastor Vargas. Have you folks been to the church tonight? I found one of the side doors open when I came in tonight. I hope someone just forgot to close it. I'll check around and talk to you later."

Dad looked at me, but he didn't say anything. Mom said, "Is it just me, or is this Christmas program creating more problems than usual? Maybe someone else should be in charge of it."

"Now, dear, if this is a problem, it has nothing to do with your program." Dad patted her arm.

I patted her other arm. The one holding a nice big bag that could be hiding presents. "You're doing a great job, Mom. Your programs are always the best."

She smiled. "I'm glad you think so, Zack. I've been meaning to tell you why I need you to be one of the wise men."

I was still trying to be nice. "Why do you need me, Mom? I'm not that wise."

Kayla agreed. "No kidding."

Mom ignored her. "Zack, I've figured out a way to borrow a special animal just for the wise men."

Suddenly, my stomach dropped into my shoes.

"Oh no. Not a . . ."

Alex interrupted. "Is it a camel, Mom?"

"Yes!" Mom was all excited. "I have a camel just for the wise men. And, Zack, you're the expert camel rider in the family. You're probably the best in the whole town!"

During my trip to Israel, my friend Achmed showed me how to ride a camel. Well, really, he drove, and I just held on. So I'm no camel expert.[*] But I guess I have been around camels more than anyone else in my school. "Mom, do you know how much trouble a camel can be?"

"You don't have to ride it or anything, Zack," Mom said. "I just want you to lead it around and make it stand still."

"That'll be hard enough," I grumbled. "But I'll do it." Actually, I kind of liked the idea. This sure wasn't going to be the same old boring Christmas program!

The next day proved that I was right. It snowed a little during the day, just enough to cover the ground. Then, that night was our first real practice. To start off, the choir practiced their songs in the fellowship hall. The rest of us sat in the

---

[*] Zack met Achmed and learned about riding camels in the book *Detective Zack and the Secrets in the Sand*.

back, wishing we were out playing in the snow.

"My dad says that Pastor Vargas thought some-one was breaking into the church," Luke whis-pered as he stared out the window. "Why would anyone do that?"

"Money," Kayla said. "Whoever stole the man-ger sold it, and now they're looking for some more valuable things to steal."

"I'm not so sure," I said. "But we do need to look for clues when we get outside." I looked around. "Where is Jodie, anyway?"

No one had seen her. I was ready to sneak out to the stable, but the singing finally stopped. "Everyone out to the stable," Mom said. "Please get your coats on before you go out. Now, remem-ber, choir, you'll be sitting on the bales of hay out in front of the stable."

Everyone swarmed out into the parking lot, trying to scrape up enough snow to make a snow-ball. It wasn't really dark, because Mom had the parking-lot lights on. As everyone milled around the bales that had been arranged into choir seats, Mom went over to one side of the stable. "Let's see if this works," she said, flipping a switch.

"Oooooh," everyone said, looking up. There, up on a tall pole over the stable, was a star shape covered with white Christmas lights. "Hey, it's just like in Bethlehem," Alex said.

The star made the whole scene seem friendly and warm. Mom directed everyone to their places to begin the skit. "Angels stay out of sight behind the stable," she repeated to the ones with wings. "The shepherds should be sitting here, and then . . ."

And then, it happened. Suddenly, Mr. DuCaut's reason for saying what he did was very clear.

"Christmas is about decorating a tree."

Christmas Clues

Even Santas get thirsty.

The tradition of Christmas trees started about four hundred years ago in Germany, probably because of a story that told about people tying apples on an evergreen tree at Christmastime.

The decorated-Christmas-tree idea came to America with German settlers in Pennsylvania.

The only thing about Christmas trees that has to do with the story of Jesus is the tradition of placing a star at the top of the tree to remind people of the star that the wise men followed.

Missing Manger Mystery

When Jodie left the practice, no one was there to pick her up. Where did she go?

Jodie was in trouble at school for having matches. She could have stolen Mrs. Antonelli's flashlight. Could she have started the fire at the stable?

Jodie says that Christmas is a waste of time. Would she start a fire and steal the manger to stop the Christmas program?

CHAPTER SIX

Footprints in the Snow

December 19

The whole scene lit up like someone had set off silent fireworks above us in the sky. Everyone's eyes turned toward the DuCauts'.

"Oooooh!"

Their whole house was covered with Christmas lights. The winking and blinking were enough to make a person dizzy. A huge Santa and his reindeer were outlined on the lawn. The roof spelled out "Merry Christmas." And above it all was a large bright star.

About a hundred times brighter than our star.

I thumped myself on the head. "So that's what I heard last night. Mr. DuCaut was putting the lights up on his house. He was probably dragging an extension cord across the roof."

"Well," Mom said slowly, "isn't that nice. And now we have more light to practice by. Come on, now, you shepherds are supposed to sit here."

The shepherds with their staffs sat on a circle of hay bales and watched the lights at the DuCauts. "The angels are going to have a hard time outshining that," Luke said.

Meanwhile, Mom got Mary and Joseph started. They were supposed to walk out from the darkness behind the church to the stable. "Remember, when you hear Mrs. Lin read the words 'And Joseph also went up from Galilee,' you start walking."

"What about the donkey?" Kayla asked.

"If the donkey behaves, you'll be riding it, and Joseph will be holding the reins as he walks. For now, just walk. Wise men, I need you over here."

We were supposed to wait at the back of the church too. "I want the three of you out of sight, but watching."

I looked at Luke. Luke looked at me. "Uh, Mom," I started to say, looking at Luke, "there's only two . . ." Then I glanced behind us. There was Jodie. "How do you keep doing that?" I groaned.

"I'm fast." That's all she would say.

Mom ignored us. "Zack, if we can get the camel

to cooperate, I want you to lead it. Jodie and Luke, you'll be walking beside it. Be sure to walk on the side next to the parking lot so people can see you. Wait for the words 'After Jesus was born in Bethlehem in Judea.' Then start toward the stable. Any questions?"

Luke had a question. "What are we going to do for a manger, since the other one was stolen?"

Mom sighed. "I don't know. Don't worry about it for now." But you could tell that she was worried about it. She looked back toward the stable. "No, no, there will be no flying by any angels in this program. Get down from there." With a big sigh, she headed back.

We kicked snow around for a few minutes while we waited. Then Luke started trying to make giant chicken footprints. "A giant Christmas chicken is stalking the town," he cackled.

"That would be scary." I rubbed my head. Even Jodie smiled about that one. Then an idea hit me so fast I said it without thinking. "Hey, this is a great chance to look for clues that someone is breaking into the church." As soon as I said it, I wished I hadn't.

Luke didn't think either. "That's right! We were going to look for clues about the missing manger anyway." He turned to look at the stable and finally remembered that Jodie was standing there. And that she was one of our suspects.

I tried to think fast. "But the batteries in my flashlight are dead, so we'll have to do it later."

Jodie's face had questions written all over it, but she didn't say anything.

"Oh, all right," Luke agreed. "We'll do it later." We started to walk away.

"I have a flashlight," Jodie said. "Let's go."

What could we do? I shrugged at Luke, and we followed her around the corner to the dark side of the church. "What are we looking for?" she asked, clicking on her light.

"Footprints," I said. "As far as I know, there weren't any meetings at the church today, so no one should have been walking around over here. And any footprints showing tonight would have to have been made since it snowed this afternoon."

We stalked slowly around the building behind the sweep of the flashlight's beam. The snow was as smooth as a blanket. But when we neared the door on that side, Jodie held up her hand. "Wait! I see footprints."

We bent down closer, trying not to trample the prints. "They're on the sidewalk that leads to the street on this side," I said.

Jodie followed them with her light all the way to the church. "They go right up to the door." She turned the other way. "And all the way to the street."

Luke stood up. "Probably the mail carrier or someone. Let's go."

I stood up too, but something about the footprints seemed strange to me. I just couldn't think of what it was.

We were halfway back around the building when I stopped. "That's it!" I shouted. Luke almost bumped into me.

"What's it?" he asked. Jodie turned back too.

"The footprints. They're only going one way!"

They looked at me like I had sprouted reindeer horns. And a very shiny nose.

"Come on, I'll show you." We ran back and stared at the marks on the sidewalk. "See, in each of these footprints, the toes are pointed toward the street. There aren't any coming in from the street."

Jodie caught it first. "So no one went in that door. But someone came out and walked to the street."

"So someone was in the church," Luke agreed. "They probably snuck out this way when people started arriving for practice."

Then, from around the other side of the church, we heard people shouting. And barking. "Come on," I said, "we'd better go see what's happening."

The first thing I noticed was that the little shepherds were the ones shouting. And laughing. A big yellow dog was the one barking. Mom was waving her arms. "Sit down, please. If everyone will sit down, I'm sure the dog will go away."

When I got close enough, I started talking to the dog. "Here, girl. Come on. Come over here so I can pet you." The dog took one look at me and ran.

She ran right to me, tongue waving and tail wagging. "What a nice, friendly dog you are," I said, patting her shiny golden fur. "Whose dog is it?" I asked Mom.

"I guess no one's," she answered. "It just showed up. Actually, it wasn't causing any trouble until the shepherds started a game of tag."

The dog looked up at me and smiled a big, goofy grin. "Well, I hope you find your way home tonight," I said. "You seem like a nice dog to have around."

"I think we've had enough practice for tonight," Mom said. "Start working on your costumes. Do you know what to wear?"

"Bathrobes," everyone said together.

On our way to the car, Luke had a question. "Do

you think Jodie could have taken the manger? Or set the fire? She sure seemed like she wanted to help."

"I know. But did you get a look at her flashlight? It was small and black. Just like Mrs. Antonelli's."

CHAPTER SEVEN

Hanging Shoes by the Window With Care

December 20

"Shhh!"

"Sorry!" Luke and I stopped talking and pulled out the books the card-catalog file had listed. "I knew the library would have information about Christmas customs in other countries," I whispered. "See, right here." I pointed. "Christmas Traditions in Europe."

Luke pointed to a chapter in his book. "Mine says 'Christmas Around the World.' This should be easy."

I got my paper out and wrote 'Social Studies' at the top. Then I turned to the section on France. "Luke," I whispered, "look at this. In France, kids don't hang stockings by the chimney. They put their shoes in front of the fireplace!"

"Shoes? The fireplace? Are you sure?"

I looked again. "Yes. Then, *Père Noël* [Pair Noel] can fill them with presents."

"Pear who?" Luke asked. "Is that like Santa Claus?"

"It says here it's French for 'Father Christmas.' Who is he?" I was getting more confused by the minute. "There must be something about this Santa Claus thing that we don't know. Well, anyway, that's one country."

Luke pointed to one in his book. "In Belgium, on the night before December 6, Saint Nicholas arrives on a boat from Spain and rides down the streets on a white horse."

"December 6?"

Luke read on. "It's like the start of the Christmas season. His servant, Black Pete, goes with him. Saint Nicholas goes down the chimney and leaves gifts in shoes by the fireplace."

"At least he goes down the chimney," I said. "Is Saint Nicholas the same as Santa?" Luke opened his mouth, but a librarian walked by, so he closed it and just shrugged.

I started reading about Germany. "Luke," I hissed, "German kids get gifts on December 6 too. But at the same time, Saint Nicholas collects their lists of things they want for Christmas."

"Boy, over here we have to mail our lists to Santa," Luke joked. "In Germany, I guess they get better service."

I ignored him. "Saint Nicholas gives the lists to the *Christkind* [Chris-kind]. That's the Christ Child."

"You mean, like Baby Jesus?"

I nodded. "The *Christkind* doesn't deliver the gifts, though. He sends the 'Christmas Man' on Christmas Eve. I guess Christmas Man must be like Father Christmas."

Luke whistled. Quietly. "Look at this! I never thought about that."

I tried to see into his book. "Look at what?"

He pointed. "In Australia, December is in the middle of summer. Many families celebrate Christmas by going to the beach."

It was hard to imagine opening presents in your swimsuit. I guess you could make a sandman instead of a snowman.

"Look what they do in Spain," I said. "It says that most homes have Nativity scenes. And after midnight mass (that's a church service) on Christmas Eve, people sing and dance in the streets."

"I guess the kids don't have to go to bed early on Christmas Eve," Luke whispered.

DETECTIVE ZACK

"Hey, wise man, listen to this. On January 5, children fill their shoes with hay for the wise men's camels. Then they leave them on a balcony or near a window. The next day is called Epiphany [E-pif-a-nee], because it is supposed to be the day that the wise men arrived in Bethlehem. According to legend, the wise men arrive during the night and fill the shoes with gifts."

"That's crazy," Luke said. Then he thought about it. "I guess it's no crazier than leaving cookies and milk for Santa."

I was writing my stuff about Spain when Luke found another interesting one.

"On each of the nine days before Christmas, some people in Mexico act out Mary and Joseph's search for a place to stay on the first Christmas Eve. Two children carrying figures of Mary and Joseph lead a kind of parade to a particular house. They knock and ask for a place to stay. At first, the people say No. But, finally, Mary and Joseph are invited in."

"They do this for nine days?" I asked. The librarian gave us another frown.

"Yes," Luke whispered. "But after each ceremony, they party and celebrate. Kids get to break piñatas and stuff like that."

That didn't sound so bad.

We scribbled for a few minutes; then I looked over my report. "We know plenty about Christmas traditions in other countries. But I still have a lot of questions."

Luke agreed. "Like why we hang stockings by the chimney, instead of shoes."

"And who all these people are who deliver Christmas presents," I added. "There's Father Christmas, *Père Noël*, Saint Nicholas, *Christkind*, Christmas Man, and, of course, Santa Claus. Let's go. Mom is supposed to pick us up on the way to practice."

We smiled at the librarian on our way out. She smiled back for once. Maybe she was happy to see us go.

It was snowing again, just little flakes and flurries. "Did you bring your flashlight?" I asked Luke in the car. "We're going to need it tonight if we're going to set a trap."

Luke groaned. "Not a trap. Zack, I remember your traps. They don't always work."

"This one can't miss," I promised.

Pastor Vargas was there to watch the practice. The dog was back too. "Whose dog is this?" he asked.

"No one seems to know," I explained as I patted her head. "She just shows up every night for practice. She must think our Nativity scene needs a dog."

He laughed. "She seems like a nice dog. I wonder what her name is?"

"Luke and I are calling her 'Nickie.' It's short for Saint Nicholas."

Soon, we were back in our spot, waiting with Jodie for our cue about Jesus being born in Bethlehem. I explained my plan while we waited. "I've been thinking about the footprints we saw in the snow."

"You mean the ones that came out of the church but didn't go in," Jodie said.

"That's just it," I agreed. "Someone did go into the church that day. But they went in before it snowed. If they have gone back in since then, we should be able to follow their prints and find out how they're getting in."

"Let's go," Luke said.

I led them along the hedge that lined the building. Since the windows are only about three feet off the ground, I suspected that the person was getting in that way.

"OK, we'll stop in front of every window. Keep your eyes open for footprints, scuffed-up dirt, broken branches, or anything that could mean a person has pushed through to get to the window."

We crept along as Luke and Jodie swept the ground with their flashlights. "I guess you're wrong," Luke said as we got to the other end of the building. "We haven't seen any kind of trail leading to the windows."

About halfway back, Jodie said, "I see some marks here like someone kicked up the snow. But they're in front of a blank wall."

Luke bent down and shone his light into the bush. "Probably just a dog or something," he said. "See, it's kind of like a tunnel for chasing rabbits."

Something about what he said make me think again. "A tunnel? Wait a minute. Luke, let me have your light." I got down and looked at the space in the bush. Then I crawled in.

"Zack, come on out of there. What are you looking for, a tunnel under the church?"

I kept going, then turned left. "Not under the church," I huffed. "Beside it. Right through the bushes." Then I stood up next to the church wall, right under the window.

"It leads all the way to there?" Jodie asked.

"Yes. And just as I thought, this window isn't locked."

"What room is that?" Luke asked.

I stared in. "The kitchen."

65

DETECTIVE ZACK

"So, what do we do now? Go tell Pastor Vargas?" Jodie asked.

"Not yet. I still have a plan." I crawled back out and started to explain my plan for locking the thieves inside by blocking the doors. But when we got to the sidewalk, I stopped. I still had Luke's light, so I shone it up and down carefully. There were new prints leading in from the street next to the ones leading out.

"These prints, the ones pointed toward the street, are from yesterday," I whispered. "The new footprints are leading into the church, and there isn't a new set leading back to the street!"

"Does that mean . . ." Jodie's head whipped around, and she stared at the church. ". . . they're still in there?"

"Christmas is about hanging your shoes by the window and waiting for the wise men."

Words to Remember

Père Noël [Pair No-el]: French for "Father Christmas" (whoever that is).

Christkind [Chris-kind]: German for the "Christ Child," or Baby Jesus.

Epiphany [E-pif-a-nee]: the last day of Christmas. It's supposed to be the day that the wise men arrived in Bethlehem.

Christmas Clues

In France, kids put their shoes in front of the fireplace, and Père Noël fills them with presents.

In Germany, Saint Nicholas gives gifts on December 6 and collects lists of things children want. He gives the lists to the Christkind, who sends the "Christmas Man" on Christmas Eve.

In Australia, December is in the middle of summer. Many families celebrate Christmas by going to the beach.

In Spain, on January 5, children fill their shoes with hay for the wise men's camels and leave them near a window. The wise men fill them with gifts.

CHAPTER EIGHT

Catching the Thieves

December 20

"Whoever has been breaking into the church must be inside right now," I whispered.

"So what do we do?" Jodie croaked. She sounded nervous all of a sudden.

"Forget the old plan," I said. "Here's a new one. I'll stay here and watch the door. Luke, you wait up by the corner in case they try to come out a different way. Jodie, you run get Pastor Vargas and bring him back here."

I don't know what Jodie told Pastor Vargas, but they were back in just a few minutes. "What is going on, Zack? Jodie insisted that you needed my help."

I explained what we had discovered. I could tell

he didn't believe me, but he agreed to go along with it. "We'll wait here by the door. Jodie and Luke will go in the fellowship-hall door and work their way back through the church, turning on lights as they go."

He sighed. "OK, if you say so."

By now, Jodie was biting her fingernails and pacing in a small circle. "Don't worry," I told her. "Just talk loud as you go, and turn on every light. Whoever it is will be looking for a quiet way to disappear."

Pastor Vargas huffed out a few breaths, and I knew he was feeling impatient. I could almost hear him roll his eyes. Finally, lights started coming on in the church.

"OK, here we go," I whispered. I strained to see the door in the darkness. I still had Luke's flashlight, but I couldn't turn it on yet.

Then Pastor Vargas grabbed my arm. "Look!" he hissed. The door was opening!

We stared as two dark forms slipped out and closed the door silently behind them. As soon as the door shut, I jumped out in front of them and aimed the light right in their eyes. "Gotcha!"

It was a man and a woman. The man's hands flew up to cover his eyes. But the woman could only turn her head away. Her hands were full of something wrapped in a towel.

Pastor Vargas was right beside me. "What were you doing in our church?" Just then, the bright light over the door came on, and Luke and Jodie stepped out behind the man and woman.

"You caught them," Luke said. "And it looks like they're stealing something besides the manger this time. I guess Kayla was right."

The man's shoulders sank, and his head hung down. He looked deflated—and embarrassed. Tears were running down the woman's face. "May we see what you have hidden there?" Pastor Vargas said firmly. "Or do I need to call the police?" The woman shot a scared look at her companion. He shrugged.

I stepped in to stare as she unwrapped the towel. "Probably, the stereo system from the youth room," Luke muttered. But when she held it up, we were all shocked.

It was a baby. And it started to cry.

Right away, Pastor Vargas's voice changed. "I'm Pastor Vargas. Please, come into my office. Let's talk about this somewhere out of the cold."

I don't know if he was inviting us, but we tagged along as he led the couple to his office and listened as the man tried to explain.

"I'm Joe Carpenter, and this is my wife, Maria,"

the man began. He smiled at the baby. "Joshua is only two months old. We moved to your town a few weeks ago because I was promised a job at the factory. But when we got here, there was no job. Then Joshua got sick, and we spent most of the money we had on the doctor and medicine."

Maria spoke up. "We don't know anyone in this town. And we didn't have anywhere to stay. So we've been sleeping in our car. It's down the street at that park."

Joe threw up his hands. "I promise we didn't steal anything. But we needed bathrooms and a warm place to wash and care for Joshua. I saw your church sitting here empty and dark most nights. Then I discovered a way to get in."

I spoke up. "Through the window. And by crawling through the bushes so no one would see your footprints."

Joe kind of smiled. "I thought it would keep anyone from finding out about us until we had enough money to rent a place."

I grinned at Luke and Jodie. *But we had found out.*

Joe went on. "Lately, we've been staying in the church a little longer in the evening. It's been so cold in the car." He looked over at the baby as he spoke. Then he looked up. "But we didn't take anything." I noticed a square bulge in his shirt pocket.

Pastor Vargas looked like he was in pain. "I'm very sorry all this has happened to you. I feel responsible. I feel like the church should have been there to help you."

Maria smiled. "Well, it was."

Luke piped up, "What about the manger?"

Pastor Vargas frowned. "Our Christmas manger disappeared about the time we started suspecting someone was coming into the church. You haven't borrowed it or something?"

Joe looked at Maria. "What is a manger?"

"Kind of a small bed."

"Everything we own is in our car," Joe said. "We don't have room for anything like that."

Pastor Vargas nodded. "Let me call a few people I know. Our church helps run a shelter for people who are stuck like you. We'll find you a place to stay where Joshua can be warm all night." He glanced at me. "You kids had better get back to your program."

"What kind of program is it?" Maria asked. She turned a little red. "I've watched through the window a few times."

"A live Nativity scene. You know, about when Jesus was born."

She looked blank.

"A Christmas program," I said.

"Oh, that's nice," she said. "Where will you put the tree?"

Then her husband called her, and we slipped out the door. "She acted like she didn't know anything about Jesus," Luke said.

"Some people don't," I said, thinking about Bobby. "But they seem nice. I don't think they stole the manger."

Jodie snorted. "People aren't always what they seem to be. They could have stolen it and sold it for money, just like Mrs. Hopkins said." She walked on ahead, and I slowed down to talk to Luke.

"Did you notice that Mr. Carpenter had a pack of cigarettes in his pocket?"

Luke shook his head. "So what?"

"Then he must carry matches or a lighter. The firefighter said that a homeless person might have set the fire to keep warm. Maybe he did steal the manger."

We got back to the stable just as a truck pulling a long trailer pulled up. A man in boots hopped out. "Is this the spot for the Christmas program?" he asked.

"Yes," Mom answered. "Can I help you?"

Baaa! Mooo! The man had to wait for the noise

from the trailer to die down. "I got your animals." He grinned. "Where would you like them?"

"My animals! You aren't supposed to deliver them until the day before Christmas."

The man scratched his head. "That's what the boss said. But then he decided to go visit his family out of town. Now he says if you don't get them tonight, you won't get them at all."

Mom put her hands on her head. "OK, OK. Set up the pen over there."

Everyone crowded around as the man and his helper set up a metal fence in a big square. The animals kept bleating and mooing and braying until they were finally led down the ramp out of the trailer. One donkey, one small cow, and two sheep looked very strange standing in the church yard.

"The boss sent along some extra hay for them," the man told Mom as he and his helper stacked it near the fence. "We'll be back the day after Christmas."

"Well," Mom said to us, "meet your partners in the Christmas play." She leaned over to scratch the donkey's ears.

I could have warned her about that.

"Heehaw, heehaw!" the donkey brayed in her face.

CHAPTER NINE

A Visit With Santa

December 21

I don't like to go shopping, but when you aren't sure your parents have bought all your presents, you have to tag along.

Mom and Dad started shopping at the Bon Charge. Kayla ran to look for something she wanted to hint about. Alex hung around in case there was a chance he could whine them into buying something for him on the spot.

Luke told me that his family was going to the mall too, but since I hadn't seen him, I was wandering around alone. I saw a store that sold stationery, so I stopped to look around for clues.

"Does your store print stationery?" I asked the clerk.

He looked me over. "Yes, and it makes a fine gift for Christmas. How much paper would you need?"

"Oh no," I answered. "I'm looking for a business that uses a certain kind of stationery. It's kind of a light-blue-with-speckles color."

"Red speckles?" he asked halfheartedly. I guess he already figured that I wasn't buying anything.

"No, white. For a business on State Street."

He shook his head as he turned back to whatever he was doing behind the counter. "We have only red speckles."

I walked out and almost walked into Jodie. She was following along about half a store behind her family.

I reached out to tap her on the shoulder and say Hi. But her father's voice stopped me.

"Jodie, get up here with the rest of us. You keep falling behind like that, and the next thing I know, we'll have to spend the rest of the evening looking for you." He waited and snatched her arm as she came near.

"Dad, why do we have to buy a robe? I don't want to be in that Christmas program anyway." Somehow, Jodie's voice sounded different than it did on the playground.

I stepped back against the store window and watched them in the reflection.

A Visit With Santa

He threw up his hands in the air. "How many times do I have to tell you? You will be in that play! Goodness knows, you can't sing or play the piano like your sister. I don't care if the program's about Christmas or the Easter bunny. You can stand there in a robe and play your part. Give your mother and me something to be proud of, for once."

Jodie turned away from her dad and faced my direction. I ducked back into the store. After counting to twenty, I walked out like I didn't know they were anywhere around. And they weren't. Jodie and her family were gone.

I walked on toward the mall center, where the same Santa sat in front of a long line of little kids. I climbed to the upper-level balcony and had an orange juice while I watched the shoppers.

Then a hand hit my shoulder. It was Luke. "Hey, that looks like my face after all my presents are open. What's going on?"

I shrugged. "I just overheard Jodie's dad telling her how dumb she is. And he's forcing her to be in the program. No wonder she hates Christmas."

"Someone hates Christmas?"

I didn't recognize the voice. So when I turned around, I was shocked to see a man dressed in a red-and-white suit, holding a cup of orange juice.

It was my friend, Santa!

"May I join you?" he asked. We both just nodded. I looked over the balcony and saw the "Closed" sign on Santa's chair. Even though we both knew he was just a guy in a Santa suit, it was weird sitting at a table drinking orange juice with Santa.

He took a long sip, then looked at us over the top of his round glasses. "You two don't seem real happy, considering what time of year this is. Have you already been so naughty that Santa will have to cross you off his list?"

"No," I said. "We just feel bad for a friend who is having a terrible Christmas."

Luke changed the subject. "What do you do in real life? I mean, you can't be a Santa all year long."

Santa raised a bushy white eyebrow. "You don't believe in Santa Claus, do you?"

Luke laughed. "Sorry."

Santa sighed. "Well, too bad for you. Actually, I'm retired. I used to teach school, but I've been Santa every Christmas for about ten years. Since this is my real hair and beard, I fit the part pretty well."

"We've been trying to figure out where Santa came from," I said. "Then we found out that there's more than just Santa. There's Saint Nicholas, Father Christmas, *Père Noël*, and Christmas Man. It's pretty confusing."

"That's what I thought too," Santa said. "But I searched out the answers so I could explain it to my students." He took another drink and waved at a little kid who was pointing and staring. "It seems there really was a Saint Nicholas. He was a real person who lived in the country of Turkey. He was a Catholic [kath-uh-lick] priest and was known for giving gifts."

"So he started the idea of giving gifts at Christmastime?" Luke asked.

Santa frowned. "No, actually, the custom of giving gifts on a special day in winter was practiced before people in that part of the world even heard about Jesus. After the story of Jesus was well known and churches were built in most towns, the good Saint Nicholas became a symbol of giving gifts on a special day to celebrate Jesus' birth."

I whipped out my notebook (a good detective always has paper and something to write with). "So after people learned about Jesus, they decided to celebrate His birthday during the winter? And give gifts, like they had done before?"

"Right. In those early days, all churches were joined together and led by priests of the Roman

81

Catholic Church. Then, the Reformation [ref-or-may-shun] came. People began to rebel against the Catholic system and set up churches separate from it. It was like a long war."

Santa was starting to sound an awful lot like the teacher he used to be.

"Now that they were separate, the people in the new churches didn't want to talk about a Catholic saint as a symbol of giving. So they made up some new people to use as symbols. In England, the new person was called 'Father Christmas.' In France, he was known as *'Père Noël.'* "

I was writing like crazy. "Hold on. Is this the same guy they call 'Christmas Man' in Germany?"

Santa waved at some more staring kids and went on. "Yes. Also in Germany, *Christkind* [Christ Child] sends gifts at Christmastime. From that comes another name for Santa—Kris Kringle. Saint Nicholas remained popular with the Dutch people of the Netherlands. In their language, he was known as Sinter-klaas."

"Now, we're getting close," Luke interrupted.

Santa went on. "Many of the English settlers to America lived near Dutch settlers and adopted their legends. English-speaking children called the person who brought gifts 'Santa Claus.' "

A thought struck me. "Americans adopted a lot

of customs from other countries."

The teacher came out again. Santa said, "That's because most Americans were from other countries. And the kind of person who was willing to move to a new land was willing to learn from others around him. That's what made America a great country."

Luke was worried about other important things. "So where did Santa's elves come from?"

Our Santa laughed. "The Santa Claus of early America was very different from this," he said, pointing to his red suit. "Until the 1800s, people pictured Saint Nicholas as a tall, thin, stately man who wore bishop's robes and rode a white horse. Father Christmas in England is still described that way today.

"Then, almost two hundred years ago, a writer described Saint Nicholas [Santa Claus] as a stout, jolly man who wore a broad hat and huge breeches [pants] and smoked a long pipe. This Santa rode over the treetops in a wagon and filled children's stockings with presents."

"Wait a minute," I said. "Why does everyone else in the world put shoes out for gifts and Americans hang up stockings?"

He shrugged. "No one seems to know for certain. Anyway, it was that ' 'Twas the Night Before

Christmas' poem that changed things. In many ways, that poem created Christmas as we celebrate it today. It was the first mention of a sleigh and eight flying reindeer."

"Yeah," Luke joined in. "There's Dasher and Dancer and Prancer and . . . Dixon?"

Santa went on. "It was the first mention of Santa's red nose and his visit on Christmas Eve. In Belgium and the Netherlands, Saint Nicholas visits on December 5—Saint Nicholas Eve."

"That's right," I remembered. "And in Spain, kids get presents in their shoes on January 5."

Santa continued. "A man who drew cartoons for newspapers in the 1860s drew pictures of Santa with a beard, working in a toy shop, driving a sleigh and reindeer, and putting toys in stockings hung over the fireplace. When he was through, the modern legend of Santa Claus was complete."

He pushed up a red sleeve and looked at his watch. "Well, break time's over. I have to go make some more kids smile. See you guys later. Maybe on Christmas Eve!" With a smile and a ho-ho-ho, he was gone.

Just then, Alex ran up. "Zack, come on! We have to go!"

I put away my notebook. "What's the rush?"

"Mom says your camel's here."

> **"Christmas is about a visit from Saint . . . Father . . . *Père* . . . Santa . . . Kris . . . from somebody!"**

Words to Remember

Reformation: When people stopped following the Catholic Church and started new churches.

Kris Kringle: A name for Santa that comes from the German word *Christkind* [Christ Child].

Sinter-klaas: Dutch word for Saint Nicholas that English people pronounced as "Santa Claus."

Christmas Clues

There was a real Saint Nicholas who lived a long time ago. He was a Catholic priest known for giving gifts.

When the Reformation came, people in the new churches made up a new person to give gifts. Different countries made up different legends.

The traditions about Santa Claus's reindeer and toy factory at the North Pole came from cartoonists and the poem "'Twas the Night Before Christmas."

CHAPTER TEN

Old Baggy Bones

December 21, 22

When we pulled into the church parking lot, I could see the camel walking down a ramp out of a trailer. Pastor Vargas was there watching as the man led the camel over to the fenced pen.

"It's a good thing you called," he said to Mom. "I thought the camel wasn't coming until Christmas Eve."

Mom threw up her hands. "Me too. But that's what I thought about the other animals."

I heard a sound from the stable and looked over as Nickie crawled out from between two of the bales stacked against the back wall. "Here, girl," I called to the gold-colored dog. She ran to me. "So that's where you're sleeping these days. Where are you getting food to eat?"

Nickie refused to say.

"Will the camel get along with the other animals?" Mom asked the camel man.

"Camels are social animals," the man said. "There should be no problem. Who's going to be the camel driver here?"

Everyone pointed at me.

The man blinked twice. "We'll leave the halter on, and when you're ready to lead Old Baggy Bones around, you can just hook up this rope to the halter and go. She's old and slow and doesn't care much about hurrying. Take good care of her for me."

He turned and leaned over the fence where Old Baggy Bones had managed to grab a mouthful of hay from the trough. "Behave yourself, old girl," he said. "I'll be back to get you soon."

Old Baggy Bones looked up at him and paused for a second between chews. I guess that was her way of saying goodbye.

As we stood and watched Kayla and Alex pet the animals for a minute, two cars pulled into the parking lot. The people drove through slowly, pointing at the lights on the DuCauts' house. When they saw the camel, they pointed at that too.

As they drove away, Pastor Vargas had an idea. "Since we have all the animals here anyway, why don't we do a live Nativity scene for a couple of nights before the program? You know, people could drive by and look at the scene with all the animals."

Dad nodded his head. "People are driving by all the time to see that house. If we had the stable scene set up for a couple of hours each evening, we could use signs to invite everyone to the real program on Christmas Eve."

We all looked at Mom. She shook her head slowly, like it was all a bad dream. "OK," she finally said, "we could stay set up after practice for two nights before the program. But the scene wouldn't include the shepherd-and-angel choir. Those children would have to go home."

Dad and Pastor Vargas nodded. "Oh yes. Certainly."

"And," she added, "no child is going to want to sit in place in the cold for two hours. Certain adults . . ." she stared pointedly at the two of them, ". . . would have to be here the whole time to make sure everything is under control."

"Oh yes. Of course. Certainly," they agreed.

"Hey," I said, since they were ignoring me, "how I am supposed to find the missing manger if I have to stand around being a wise man every night?"

Dad frowned. "It's probably gone for good, son. Do you think those homeless people could have taken it?" he asked the pastor.

Pastor Vargas sighed. "I don't know. I don't think so, but you never know for sure with people. I invited them to the program. They seem to know very little about the Bible."

"What are we using for a manger?" Mom asked. "We still need something to put a baby in."

"I'll nail one together for you," Dad said.

"You will?" Mom asked. Dad wasn't exactly known for his ability to build things. Usually when he swung a hammer, the nails that got hit were on the ends of his fingers. Or someone else's fingers. "Maybe Zack will help you."

"Me?" I said. "Why risk my life?"

Nobody listened.

*   *   *   *

Today was the last day of school before Christmas vacation. "So if we were in Australia, we'd all be headed for the beach." Luke finished his report on Christmas traditions and sat down.

"Very good, Luke," Mrs. Lin said. "Zack, you're next."

I told them all about the traditions in Spain and

France and Germany. "So tell your parents you want to celebrate Christmas like kids do in other countries. You want presents on December 6 and December 25 and January 5."

Even Jodie laughed a little.

After everyone had given their reports, Mrs. Lin gave us one last assignment in math. Of course, I had to sharpen my pencil before I could get started. Luke was at the pencil sharpener when I got there. I waited.

"What are you doing?" I finally hissed.

"I'm making a short pencil out of a long one. The point keeps breaking." I was trying to help him (OK, maybe we were goofing off a little), when Mrs. Antonelli stuck her head in the door. "I need some help carrying a few boxes down to the basement," she said to Mrs. Lin. "Are any of your students finished with their work?"

Mrs. Lin looked around. "Zack and Luke don't seem to be busy. They would be happy to volunteer."

Luke started to protest. "But . . . I was . . . OK." We really didn't mind.

"I hope the boxes aren't too heavy," Luke said as we followed Mrs. Antonelli back to her office. "We need all our strength to hold onto that camel tonight at the Nativity scene." I had to laugh. Old

Baggy Bones had about as much energy as a brick.

"It's just three small boxes of papers we need to keep," Mrs. Antonelli said. "I'll even carry one so we can do it in one trip." She closed the lid on a box labeled "Letters From Parents" and handed it to Luke. I got the one labeled "Reports."

As we walked, Mrs. Antonelli asked, "What will you boys be doing for the holidays this year?"

"I want to have three Christmases, like Zack said in his report," Luke announced. Of course, he had to explain about the traditions in Spain and France and Germany.

She laughed as she opened the basement storage-room door and set her box on a shelf. "My husband's grandmother was from Italy. Every Christmas, she would tell her grandchildren about La Befana [la beh-fawna]."

Luke and I looked at each other. "Who?"

She laughed. "According to the legend, when the wise men started their search for the Bambino [bam-bee-no]—that's what she called the Baby Jesus—they invited La Befana to join them. She refused, saying she was too busy and had to clean her house. So she missed seeing the Bambino. Now, each year on the eve of Epiphany, La Befana goes from house to house, leaving gifts and looking for the Christ Child."

Luke and I were both so smart that we had been standing there holding our boxes while we listened. I guess we both figured that out at the same time, because when I turned to set my box down, he was turning too.

"Watch out!" We collided. I held onto my box, but Luke's slipped to the floor. Papers spilled all over. "Sorry about that, Mrs. Antonelli," I said. "We'll get them all picked up."

She smiled and shook her head.

Just as we stuffed the last letter back into the box and Luke slapped the lid on, I saw a flash of color.

Light-blue-with-speckles color, to be exact.

"Christmas is about not having the time to look for Baby Jesus."

Words to Remember

La Befana: An Italian legend of a woman who was invited to go with the wise men. She didn't.

Bambino: The Italian name for Baby Jesus.

Christmas Clues

Italian kids get gifts from La Befana on January 5, when she goes from house to house looking for the Christ Child.

Missing Manger Mystery

I saw a piece of light-blue-with-speckles paper in one of Mrs. Antonelli's boxes. Now, if I can just get my hands on it!

CHAPTER ELEVEN

A Cereal Bowl for Sheep

December 22

I had to see that letter! I wanted to yank the box open again, but I knew Mrs. Antonelli would never allow me to look through the school's letters from parents. I thought about knocking the box out of Luke's hands again, but he was too quick for me.

"That's more like it," he said as he set it on the shelf. "Anything else we can do for you, Mrs. Antonelli?"

"Sure," I said quickly, "we could clean up the room and straighten those messy shelves."

She glanced around the tidy room and looked at me like maybe my brain was absent for the day. "No, that's all, thanks. You two had better get back to math."

I trudged out the door and cringed when she slammed it behind us. Luke didn't seem to notice what was going on. "So, did you ever find your flashlight?" he asked her.

"No, I didn't," she answered. "I hate to think that someone might have stolen it, but I would have found it by now if I had just misplaced it."

She went on to her office, but I grabbed Luke before he went back into our class. "Did you see it?" I hissed.

"See what?"

"The letter! The one on that light-blue-with-speckles stationery."

He was confused. "Like the paper at the fire? Where did you see that?"

I pulled my hair. "In the box you carried. When it fell on the floor."

"Then why didn't you . . . oh, that's what you were trying to do. If we could have stayed in that room alone for a few minutes, we could have seen whose name was on that letter." He thought about it for a second and frowned. "Well, there's no way to get back in there. And it might not have been the same stationery, even if it was the same color."

I knew he was right. But I really wanted to see that paper.

A Cereal Bowl for Sheep

We got out of school early, so I was home in time to help Dad build the new manger. "Be careful with the hammer," Mom told him. "Be quick," she told me.

I held one end of a board while Dad measured and marked it for cutting. "Dad, I don't mean this in a bad way, but do you really think you can build a manger?"

He held up one finger and aimed at the board with the power saw. *Buzzzzack!* "Well, that's almost straight on the line," he said proudly. "Zack, you don't think I can build a manger, do you?"

I got very busy hunting for another board.

He went on. "Well, if you're thinking about a manger like the one that was stolen, you're right. But that's not a real manger."

I set the new board up on the table. "It isn't?"

"What do you think a manger is for?" he asked as he measured again.

"I guess it's to put a baby in," I said. "At least, that's all I've ever heard about a manger being used for."

He held up a finger again. *Buzzzzack!* went the saw. "Well, close enough," he said as he checked out the cut. "Zack, a manger is just a feed trough."

I just stared.

7 — D.Z.M.M.M.

"A feed trough," he repeated. "A place you put food for a cow or a donkey. They eat from it like you eat from a plate. Except you use a fork or spoon. Usually."

"Dad, are you telling me that Jesus was lying in a cereal bowl for sheep?" I couldn't believe it.

He laid the two boards across each other like an X on the workbench. "It's true. The manger where Mary laid Jesus had been slobbered on by donkeys and sheep for years."

"Yuck!" I grunted.

Dad went on as he plugged in the drill. "I imagine Joseph filled it with clean hay, and then Mary put a blanket on top of that. But the donkey probably wasn't real happy to see some baby lying across his supper table."

It made sense. After all, Mary and Joseph were staying in a stable, not a hospital. "I've never thought about it like that before. I guess I always thought the church's manger was kind of a fancy baby bed."

"Hand me those screws," Dad said. "I'm going to fool your mother this time. I'm not even using a hammer. I'm going to put the manger together with screws." He slipped a screw onto the attachment to his drill and lined up the boards.

Brrizing! The screw flew off across the room.

He put another one on. *Brrizing!* It flew right past my head.

"Be careful," he said. "And hand me some more screws." The next time, it worked. *Brrrzaw!* It sunk deep into the wood.

"Very good!" I said.

"There's nothing to it," he answered with a smile. "Now, we'll do the same thing for the other two legs." He grabbed the attached boards to set them out of the way. They didn't move. Suddenly, the smile faded. He yanked at the boards again. Nothing happened.

They were screwed to each other, all right. And to the workbench. "Problem, Dad?" I asked.

"I guess the screw was a little long," he said. "I'll just back it up a little."

I'll spare you the rest of the afternoon. Anyway, by the time we were ready to leave for practice, the new manger (who says a manger can't rock a little) was carried to the car (it was so heavy it took both of us to do that). No, it wasn't a beauty. But like Dad said, any donkey would be happy to eat from it.

Practice had a lot of problems that evening. Nickie crawled out of her place in the bales and added to the confusion. "No, no, angels in front, shepherds in back," Mom said to the choir of little kids. For about the tenth time. A little angel pulled on her sleeve. "What is it, dear?"

"I need to go to the bathroom," the angel announced. Mom looked around in a panic.

"Jodie, could you come and help me?" she called over toward us.

I don't know what surprised me more—that Mom asked Jodie to help or that Jodie went and helped her. In fact, Jodie stayed with Mom for the rest of the practice, keeping kids sitting when they were supposed to and reminding them when they were supposed to stand up.

When that was finally over, the important people put on their robes while Dad and Pastor Vargas herded the animals into place for the Nativity scene. With the donkey tied to one post and the cow tied to another, they decided to let the sheep just wander around on the straw in the stable.

Once I got Old Baggy Bones to walk over to her spot just outside the stable, she didn't move another step the whole evening. She bent down for a mouthful of hay once in a while and spent the whole evening chewing.

Dad built a fire for the shepherds in their field and sat there on the hay bales with them. Nickie lay down by the fire like she had been a sheep dog all her life.

"Here comes a car," someone hissed. We all rushed to our places. Old Baggy almost stopped chewing for a second when three people in flapping robes ran toward her.

"Luke, your turban is tilting," I whispered.

"Zack, yours is on backward," Jodie giggled. We stood near the camel and looked very wise. But after twenty or thirty cars had gone by, we just looked cold.

An old car wheezed up. "Isn't that those homeless people?" Jodie asked. "You know, the ones in the church? The woman in the front seat looks like her." We turned and looked again, but we couldn't be sure.

I couldn't take any more. "Dad, send three shepherds to take our places," I called. "We're freezing!" We handed over our turbans and scooted up to the fire.

"Was it this c-c-cold in Bethlehem?" I asked Dad between chattering teeth.

"Actually," he answered with a warm smile, "this is one of the reasons why we know that December 25 is not really Jesus' birthday."

"What?" Jodie responded. "I thought it was."

"December 25 is the date we celebrate His birthday," Dad began, "but no one knows the real date. And anyone who knows Middle East shepherds knows that when it gets this cold, sheep stay inside at night."

"So this means that there weren't really any sheep out in the field that night," Jodie said. She was almost mad about it.

Dad shook his head. "No, it means that Jesus was born either earlier that fall or later the next spring. Since the shepherds were out with their flocks at night, it couldn't have happened in December."

Jodie seemed satisfied with that. "But why did we choose December 25 then?"

"The people who first heard about Christianity were already used to celebrating a holiday at that time of year. So they changed the holiday to help them remember that Jesus had been born."

Everyone was quiet for a few moments.

"Look at that," Luke said after he stopped shivering. "The stars are sparkling like diamonds."

We all looked up for a minute. "You know," I said, "this is the first time I've ever really thought about what it was like when Jesus was born. It was dark out in the fields where those shepherds were. And they didn't have flashlights."

Jodie glanced at me, then looked back up.

I went on. "And those wise men traveled a long way across the desert because they believed in a star. Then, to imagine that Jesus was King of the universe one day and lying in an animal feed trough the next—it's almost too much to believe."

It was quiet for a minute; then Jodie asked, "Well, do you?"

"Do I what?"

She stared at me. "Do you really believe that Jesus was born on earth, with the shepherds and the angels and the star? Do you think all this really happened?"

I looked around at the stable and the camel and the fire. "Yes. I believe it did."

Her next words were like a whisper. "Why would Jesus do a thing like that?"

"Christmas is about shepherds sitting in the dark, wise men wandering across the desert, and God coming down to earth—to a stable."

Christmas Clues

A manger is just a feed trough for animals, not a bed.

The shepherds wouldn't have been out in the fields at night in December. So Jesus was born in the late fall or early spring, not in the middle of winter.

We celebrate Christmas on December 25 because the first Christians were used to celebrating a holiday then. They changed it into a new holiday about Jesus.

It's hard to believe that Jesus would come and be born in a stable. If He did, He must really love us a lot. I believe He did.

CHAPTER TWELVE

Practice Disaster

December 23

It wasn't even dark yet when we got to the stable for the dress rehearsal. Nickie came out of her hiding place and stretched like she had been sleeping all day.

"Well, hello, Nickie," I said as I scratched behind her ears. I noticed some dark patches on her coat. "What is this?" I brushed at them. They felt like hair or some kind of fiber. "Have you been fighting with a black-haired dog?"

Nickie wouldn't say.

By the time the other kids began showing up, Old Baggy was tied up behind the church along with the donkey. The cow and the sheep were in place in the stable. Nickie settled down near the shepherds again. It seemed so peaceful.

Boy, did that change in a hurry.

Dad had a spotlight behind the bales of hay that were going to be the speaker's stand. Mrs. Lin was ready at the microphone. Mom got everyone else in their places and stood in front of the choir.

"We've been over all this before," she said. "Tonight is the dress rehearsal. A dress rehearsal is supposed to go from start to finish without stopping. Just do it the way we practiced. Everyone, listen for your cues."

Luke rubbed his hands together. "It's cold out here. I'm glad we're wearing our coats under these robes." We peeked around the corner as the choir stood to sing "O Little Town of Bethlehem."

"So far so good," Jodie whispered.

Mrs. Lin began reading. " 'And it came to pass in those days, that there went out a decree from Caesar Augustus, that all the world should be taxed.' "

"Zack," Kayla whispered from behind me, "help Joseph hold this donkey still while I get on."

By the time Kayla got settled, Jodie called, "Hurry, it's almost time." We listened to Mrs. Lin.

" 'And Joseph also went up from Galilee, out of the city of Nazareth, into Judea, unto the city of

David, which is called Bethlehem.' "

"Go, go," we whispered hoarsely. Joseph started forward across the yard, leading the donkey with the reins. Kayla was trying to balance herself by holding on with one hand. Her other hand was keeping the "expecting a baby" pillow inside her robe.

When the spotlight hit them, Joseph and the donkey stopped. Kayla's hand flew up to cover her eyes, and as soon as she let go, she tumbled off onto the ground.

"Get up and keep going," Mom called.

Dad shifted the light to the path in front of them. Kayla picked her pillow baby up and brushed it off. Then, with one leap, she hopped back on the donkey, clutching the pillow with one hand and the donkey's short mane with the other. "Let's go," she hissed at Joseph.

"I'm trying," Joseph said. "It won't move."

It was true. The donkey had decided to stay in that spot. "Joseph," Luke called, "get some hay. Go grab a handful of hay, and hold it in front of the donkey's mouth."

Joseph ran and grabbed the hay. The donkey took one sniff and reached out with a long red tongue. Joseph took a step backward. The donkey followed. In just a few more steps, they reached the corner of the stable. Mrs. Lin began reading again.

" 'And so it was, that, while they were there, the days were accomplished that she should be delivered. And she brought forth her firstborn son, and wrapped him in swaddling clothes, and laid him in a manger; because there was no room for them in the inn.' "

As she said those words, the lights in the stable came on. Then the star above the manger began to shine. In fact, it shined brighter than we had ever seen it.

For about three seconds. Then, with a loud "pop," it went out.

Mom stared at it for a second, then turned to her choir and motioned for them to rise. They were all still staring at the star. "Choir, we're singing now. Choir!"

Finally, they stood and stumbled through a really sad version of "Away in the Manger." Even Alex kept turning around to stare at the star. When they sat down, Mrs. Lin kept reading.

" 'And there were in the same country shepherds abiding in the field, keeping watch over their flock by night. And, lo, the angel of the Lord came upon them, and the glory of the Lord shone round about them: and they were sore afraid.' "

108

Practice Disaster

As Mrs. Lin read, the announcing angel was supposed to be getting in place on top of a bale of hay near the shepherds. But when the spotlight clicked on, the angel was still running toward the bale. She tried to jump up but somehow got tangled in her robe.

One part of the story seemed very real. When she tripped and came flying over the hay, the shepherds were sore afraid! At least, the one she landed on was sore—the others jumped back like they were scared to death.

I tried not to laugh. But Luke was rolling on the ground. And Jodie was snickering into her robe. Finally, I snatched my hat off the ground, covered my face, and laughed like a hyena.

The angel got up and brushed at the grass stains on her robe. "What do I do now?" she wailed.

Mom lifted her head up out of her hands. "Get back where you're supposed to be. Keep going please, Mrs. Lin."

" 'And the angel said unto them, Fear not: for, behold, I bring you good tidings of great joy, which shall be to all people. For unto you is born this day in the city of David a Saviour, which is Christ the Lord.' "

By now, the angel was back up on the bale, and the shepherds were bowed down to the ground, acting afraid. The way they kept glancing up and scooting back made it seem very real.

" 'And this shall be a sign unto you; Ye shall find the babe wrapped in swaddling clothes, lying in a manger. And suddenly there was with the angel a multitude of the heavenly host praising God, and saying . . .' "

Then Mrs. Lin stopped, and a row of five angels stepped out from behind the stable and recited, " 'Glory to God in the highest, and on earth peach, good will toward men.' "

"Did they say 'on earth peach'?" Jodie whispered.

"I think so." I looked over at Mom. She shook her head and motioned for the choir to stand. As the little kids shouted out "Hark, the Herald Angels Sing," the angels walked to the stable.

Mrs. Lin read, " 'And it came to pass, as the angels were gone away from them into heaven, the shepherds said one to another, Let us now go even unto Bethlehem, and see this thing which is come to pass, which the Lord hath made known unto us. And they came with haste, and found Mary, and Joseph, and the babe lying in a manger.' "

"We're next," Jodie whispered. I went and untied Old Baggy. We waited for the right words.

" 'Now when Jesus was born in Bethlehem of Judea in the days of Herod the king, behold, there came wise men from the east to Jerusalem, saying, Where is he that is born King of the Jews? for we have seen his star in the east, and are come to worship him.' "

"OK, here we go," I said, pulling on Old Baggy's rope. "Remember to walk slow."

The choir was singing the first verse of "We Three Kings." But when the spotlight hit us, there were only two kings. "Luke, you're on the wrong side of the camel," I hissed.

"Zack," Jodie hissed, "your hat!"

I didn't understand. I knew I had my hat on. I reached up with one hand and found my hat on—on top of my turban!

Mrs. Lin read, " 'When they heard the king, they departed; and, lo, the star, which they saw in the east, went before them, till it came and stood over where the young child was. When they saw the star, they rejoiced with exceeding great joy.' "

We arrived at the stable, and I tied Baggy up to her usual spot. Then we went to the manger and bowed down in front of it.

" 'And when they were come into the house, they saw the young child with Mary his mother, and fell down, and worshipped him: and when they had opened their treasures, they presented to him gifts; gold, and frankincense, and myrrh.' "

We set our gift boxes beside the manger and stepped back against the wall. The choir sang "Silent Night," and it almost sounded right.

"OK," Mom told the choir, "now you walk through and see Baby Jesus. Then go out to the side."

The kids were in no hurry to see a plastic doll. Then, someone pushed a little, and Alex called out, "Hey, me first!"

Suddenly, everyone wanted to be in front. "Me first! No, me!" The little crowd rushed toward the stable. As they got closer, it turned into a brawl. Shepherds shoving angels, angels kicking shepherds. It was awful.

The sheep got very nervous. When someone bumped one, they both ran. The donkey brayed and kicked. The cow mooed and pulled at the rope. Nickie started barking. Old Baggy stopped chewing.

Mom waded into the fight, pulling kids out and setting them off to the side. Jodie tossed her turban off and helped. I shouted at Luke, "Grab the sheep!"

He dove at one, but it gave him the slip, and he ended up eating straw. I lunged at it as it went by and managed to hang on. But I couldn't stop it.

"Whoaa!" I shouted as it dragged me around the stable. Finally, Dad caught up and stopped us both.

When the shouting stopped and the dust settled, there wasn't a clean robe in sight. Most of the dirty little faces were streaked with tears. Including Mom's.

"Well," she finally said, "I guess that's enough rehearsing for tonight. Let's all go home before something else happens."

Just then, two cars pulled up nearby. The first one was filled with people admiring the lights at the DuCauts'. The front window was rolled down. The people glanced at us. "If I were a wise man," one of them said as they drove away, "I think I'd head for the house next door."

Like we didn't feel bad enough already.

The next car was a white van. "I'll be right there," Jodie shouted to her parents inside. This time, I was close enough to read the message on the van door.

MCKANE MUSIC
FINE MUSIC, FINE INSTRUMENTS
SERVING YOU AT 201 STATE STREET

I looked away, but something about it tickled my brain. I looked back one more time, and it hit me.

113

CHAPTER THIRTEEN

Surprise in the Stable

Christmas Eve

I yanked my robe open and reached into my coat pocket. The folded-up, burned light-blue-with-speckles paper was still there. Holding it up to the light, I could still see the letters *M-E-N-T-S* and the words *STATE STREET*. It fit the words on the McKane van exactly.

"Jodie did it," I whispered to myself. I counted on my fingers. "She had matches, she didn't want to be in the program, she was alone outside the church just before the fire started, and the paper burned was stationery from her family."

I turned and watched her talking to my mom and brushing off one of the little shepherds at the same time. *She doesn't seem like the same person,*

I thought. *Now she acts like she wants to be in the program, like she really cares about it.*

"Luke, come here," I called.

"As soon as I get this sheep back in the pen," he shouted, half out of breath from pushing the sheep while Pastor Vargas pulled on its rope.

But when he was finished, his parents were waiting, so he waved and ran to their car.

All the way home, I argued with myself. *I should tell Mom what she did. Jodie might be planning to try it again.*

Just then, I overheard what Mom was saying to Dad. "What a disaster. Thank goodness, Jodie was there. She sure has been a help. I don't know what I would have done without her."

I can't tell her. After the kind of evening she had, I can't tell her that her best helper tried to burn down the stable!

I didn't say anything. But I kept thinking. *Jodie acted like she hated Christmas and the story of Jesus. But, now, it seems like maybe she's a little interested. What will happen if I tell and she gets thrown out of the program?*

I don't know about Mom, but the closer we got to time for the program, the more nervous I felt. Finally, this afternoon, I decided I would tell Mom and let her decide what to do.

"Mom," I said as she was packing up some stuff in the kitchen, "I need to talk to you."

"OK," she said. "By the way, I invited your friend Bobby and his parents to the program tonight."

"Great," I said. I was excited to hear it, but I had so much on my mind.

"We can talk while we carry these things to the car," she added. I picked up a box and followed her out. "No, Alex," she called as soon as we got to the garage. "You can't take your sled."

"But, Mom! Dad said it might snow tonight."

She was still talking to him when the phone rang back in the kitchen. "Mom! It's for you!" Kayla called from inside.

By the time she hung up, it was time to get in the car. I stewed about it all the way to the church.

I need to tell an adult about Jodie, because starting fires is dangerous to her and others. But if her dad finds out, he will probably treat her even worse. Still, if she hid the manger nearby, we could still get it back in time for the program.

I followed Mom to the stable as soon as we got there. "Mom, I still to need to . . ."

Someone was already in the stable—the last person I wanted to see. "Jodie," Mom said, "why are you here so early?"

Jodie didn't give me time to say anything. "I need to talk to you," she said to Mom. "Here," she said, holding out her hand. Mom reached to get— a box of matches!

"Jodie?" Mom was confused. So was I.

Jodie talked fast. "I want to tell you that I'm sorry. I didn't want to be in the program at first, but my dad made me. We're not getting along too well right now." She brushed back a tear.

"Anyway, I had these matches, and I was out here waiting for him that night, and starting a fire seemed like a good way to get out of the program and get back at him. Now, I'm glad it didn't work."

"Oh, sweetheart, I'm so sorry," Mom said as she reached to hug Jodie.

"You're not mad?" Jodie almost whispered.

Mom almost laughed. "No. A little confused, but not mad. I like you, Jodie. You've been such a big help to me this week. I want to be your friend."

Jodie hugged her again. "Thank you for being so nice to me, for picking me to be a wise person, and for letting me help you." She looked over at me. "And thank you for treating me like a friend. I don't have too many of those."

What could I say? "You're a great wise person. And a pretty good detective. Uh, did you see what happened to the manger?"

"No, I didn't. I don't know who took it." She backed away and wiped her eyes. "The way Christians treat each other at my house sometimes, I don't want anything to do with God most of the time. But if believing in Him is what makes your family so nice, then I want to learn more about Him."

Mom stared after her as she walked away. I walked over and hugged her. "Zack, that was a real Christmas miracle. Showing someone love is what Christmas is all about." She wiped her eyes. "Now, what did you need to talk to me about?"

I laughed. "Oh, nothing, really. It's not important now. I'm sorry I didn't find the manger."

"Don't worry about that. The manger may have been valuable, but it's not worth nearly as much as a person. Like Jodie. And you."

Well, that was enough of the mushy stuff, so I got busy raking fresh hay around. With big animals, you always need a shovel and fresh hay. Nickie's head popped out from between the bales. "There you are," I said, stopping to pet her. "How do you like that hay palace?"

She didn't say.

"Is anyone here?" a voice called from the front. I went out just as Mom came back from the car.

Surprise in the Stable

"Oh, hello again, Mr. DuCaut," Mom said. "Tonight's the big program."

He nodded. "That's why I'm here."

Oh no, I thought, *he's here to complain about the animals or the noise.*

"I saw what happened last night," he went on. "I'm here to offer you my star for your program."

Mom's mouth fell open. "Really?"

He shrugged. "We were planning to turn the lights off anyway and come over to watch."

By the time everyone began arriving, Dad and Mr. DuCaut had the new star in place. We rushed around getting the animals in place.

Kayla complained, "Mom, this plastic doll looks terrible. It doesn't even seem like a real baby."

Mom rushed by. "I'm sorry, dear, but all the Rent-a-Baby places were closed today."

Pastor Vargas happened to be going by. "I have an idea," he said. Then he went off into the crowd.

I got my turban on without the hat and joined Jodie and Luke next to Old Baggy. "I hope things go better tonight," Luke said.

"I don't see how they could go much worse," Jodie said with a laugh.

Joseph and Kayla were practicing getting on and off the donkey. "I brought hay this time," Joseph said, holding up a handful.

"Look!" I pointed up to the sky. "It's snowing!" The white flakes fell softly over everything.

The choir began singing, and we peeked around the corner to watch. Then we heard Mrs. Lin's voice. " 'And Joseph also went up from Galilee, out of the city of Nazareth, into Judea, unto the city of David, which is called Bethlehem.' "

"Here we go," Kayla said. Joseph pulled the hay out and held it in front of the donkey.

"Good luck," Jodie whispered as they started off. We held our breath when the spotlight came on, but the donkey never slowed down. In a minute they disappeared behind the stable.

"I hope they fixed the lights on the star," Luke mumbled.

"Just watch," I said. The stable light came on, and the crowd said, "Ahhh!"

Then someone turned on the star. "Ooooh," everyone said.

"Wow! Where'd we get that light?" Luke asked. "It's as bright as . . . Hey, it *is* the star from the house next door."

The choir sang "Away in the Manger." I pointed toward the shepherds. "Here comes the tricky part." With the extra light of the star, we could see the announcing angel heading for her spot. "Come on, come on. Get up on the bale."

CHAPTER FOURTEEN

Mangers and Miracles

Christmas Eve

" '. . . and the glory of the Lord shone round about them: and they were sore afraid.' "

The light came on, and the angel was there. The shepherds did a good job of looking scared. They'd had a lot of practice.

We watched as the other announcing angels lined up and spoke. "No peaches this time," Jodie said under her breath. When they went into the manger and when the shepherds followed them in, the crowd seemed to laugh a little.

"What's going on?" Jodie asked. I just shrugged. "We're next," she whispered. I got Old Baggy, and we stood waiting.

" 'Where is he that is born King of the Jews?

for we have seen his star in the east, and are come to worship him.' "

The crowd said, "Oooh," when they saw the camel, but we were the ones who were surprised when we got to the stable. This time, Nickie was lying beside the manger as if she were guarding it.

And the baby in the manger was a real baby!

A little hand reached up to grab Kayla's finger. "Where did you get that?" I whispered when we knelt down in front of the manger.

"It's Joshua," she whispered back, trying not to move her lips. "You know, the homeless people's baby."

We moved back by the wall while the choir sang "Silent Night." But something about it seemed magical to me. Little Joshua's parents had come to town and found no room to live in either. But just like Baby Jesus, God had a plan to care for them. He was using us, just like He had used the angels and shepherds and wise men when Jesus was born.

I was watching when Mom turned the first group of choir kids loose to come into the stable, just in case the arguing started. But when they saw the baby, everything changed.

"It's a real baby!" one of them whispered louder than I usually talk.

The crowd said, "Ahhhh!"

The kids crowded up to the edge of the manger in their robes, full of smiles. Then they moved away, whispering excitedly.

It was amazing.

We stayed in our places while Pastor Vargas stood to say a few words. "The children have discovered the truth about Christmas. Yes, it was a real baby in the manger that night in Bethlehem. Jesus really came to be with us, to show us how much God loves us."

He looked over the crowd. "My favorite Christmas verse is not one from the story we heard tonight. It says, 'For God so loved the world, that he gave his only begotten Son.' God loved, so He gave. That's what Christmas is all about—loving and giving."

After the prayer, people crowded forward and took about four thousand pictures. I hadn't seen that many flashes since the Fourth of July. Finally, we were finished.

"You guys did a wonderful job," Mom said to us all. "It was perfect. I'm so proud of you all." It felt great to hear that. Jodie looked happier than I had ever seen her.

The Carpenters came up to get little Joshua. "This was so special," Maria said. "Thank you so much for what you've done for us. Joe has a job now, and we're going to make it—thanks to the people at this church. Now I understand a little more about what makes you all so kind."

After they were gone, Pastor Vargas said, "I think they'll be coming to our church next week. Isn't it amazing how God used this program? And these kids?"

God wasn't through yet.

Bobby and his parents came up. "Hey, man, you were great," Bobby said. "You really do know how to handle a camel." He patted Old Baggy.

"It was a beautiful program," his mom told my mom. "Thanks so much for inviting us."

His dad shook hands with Pastor Vargas. "We both went to church when we were children, but we have never taken our son. Maybe it's time we did."

"You'll always be welcome here," Pastor Vargas said.

I just stared after them when they walked away. It was almost too much. I looked at Mom. "Another Christmas miracle!" She nodded and blinked back tears.

Mrs. Antonelli came by to say how proud she was of us. I noticed a black flashlight in her hand. "Did you get it back?" I asked.

"Yes," she said, and we both glanced over at Jodie. "And your mother spoke to me."

I stepped closer and whispered, "Will you be able to help her? I mean, with her dad and everything?"

"I'll try," she said. "She's lucky to have friends like you and your mother."

I just smiled. By now, almost everyone was gone. I wandered over by the manger to pet Nickie. "You did a good job tonight too," I said, brushing some more of the black fibers off her coat. Alex came in, exhausted from a snowball fight. He tried to lie in the manger.

"It's just not big enough," he moaned. "I wish I could sleep in between the bales of hay like Nickie does."

I laughed. "Nickie couldn't either unless there was an open space in there." All of a sudden, a flash went off in my brain.

"That's it!" I shouted.

Everyone standing around—Mom, Dad, Luke, Jodie, the Hopkins, Pastor Vargas—turned to stare at me. "What's it?" Mom asked.

"The missing manger." I ran over to the spot where Nickie slept and started knocking bales onto the ground.

"Zack, what are you doing?" Dad asked.

I answered while I shoved. "Pastor Vargas, what did you do with the manger when Mrs. Hopkins gave it to you?"

"I didn't do anything with it. I just set it against the wall," he answered.

Mr. Hopkins spoke up. "It wasn't there when I unloaded the hay. I know what that manger looks like. I would have seen it."

Mom was remembering. "But it was wrapped up."

"That's right," I said, pushing the last bale away. "With a black blanket." I reached down and pulled up one corner of the blanket.

"That's my blanket!" Mrs. Hopkins cried.

I bent down and pushed back the blanket. "And here's your manger."

Everyone rushed up, talking at the same time. "Is the manger OK? How did this happen? How did you figure it out?"

Mr. Hopkins just stared. "We never saw it in the dark. We just stacked the hay all around it."

Mrs. Hopkins grabbed the manger to inspect it. Pastor Vargas looked even happier than before. Luke grabbed my arm. "How did you know?"

I pointed to Nickie. "You know she's been sleeping in here, between the bales. And you've seen the black stuff on her coat." He nodded. "I never put the two together until I was talking to Alex a minute ago."

Alex looked proud. "I helped solve the mystery!"

I tried to explain. "I realized that there had to be an open spot where Nickie was sleeping. And then I remembered that the manger had been wrapped in a black blanket."

"Nickie was sleeping on that blanket, next to the manger, all this time," Jodie finished it for me. "That's amazing."

It was amazing. The whole night had been amazing. Bobby and his family might come to church. The homeless family had a home and friends who cared. And Jodie wanted to know more about God's love.

Maybe that's what Christmas is really all about. All the strange traditions, all the Santa Clauses and Father Christmases and Christmas trees and everything that people do at Christmastime— all of them are just stories or activities that remind people that they are loved. By their family, by their friends, and most of all, by God.

I guess that's what Christmas is really about— the amazing things God does to show people how much He loves them. And what's really amazing is—He lets us help.

"Christmas is about loving and giving."

Christmas Clues

When you can see that there was a real baby in the manger in Bethlehem, you can see that Jesus really did come to earth.

Even with all the traditions that have nothing to do with the Bible story, celebrating Christmas with love can change people's lives and make them happy.

All the stories of Santas and stockings and shoes and everything else were just made up to remind people that they are loved. By their family, by their friends, and most of all, by God.

Missing Manger Mystery

Jodie seems like a different person today—a happier one.

Nickie knew where the missing manger was all the time. But you know her—she didn't say a word!

My Christmas list(now that the program is over)

A new flashlight
A new notebook
Nickie (can we take her home, Mom?)